Candy-Coated Courtship

By Meyari McFarland

Candy-Coated Courtship

This book is also available in ebook format on Amazon.com, Barnes & Noble, Smashwords.com, and other book retailers.

ISBN-978-1-939906-97-7

Cover Art: © Svetlanakroitor | Dreamstime.com -
A Cup Of Herbal Tea, A Plate Of Fresh Pastry, Yellow Autumn Leaves,
Ripe Red Currants And Garden Flowers On A Wooden Surface Photo

Printed in the U.S.A

Dedication

This story is dedicated to Cathy for letting me go, to JC for being my friend, and all the lovers of ladies everywhere.

Other Books by Meyari McFarland:

Table of Contents

Candy-Coated Courtship

Amirah stopped just inside the door and shifted to the left so that other people could pass her by. She shut her eyes, breathed deep. Yeast, sugar, the acrid bright smell of fresh green tea, the sort that tasted like grass on your tongue and cloyed the back of your throat so badly that you took another drink in the vain hope that the tea would make you less thirsty instead of more. Under that was chocolate, thick and rich, and wax from the squeaking floors that made her heels slip and tremble every time she walked in.

Home.

Or as close to home as Amirah was going to get while away at college. When her parents visited she would bring Mother here, would pull her to the left so that they could breathe together and remember Grandmother's kitchen, the smell of mint tea and bread and thick spicy kahari. It was different from here, from Candy Courtship, but the smells were so thick that Amirah loved it. Mother would too.

Father would forge straight for the counter, tapping it with his blunt fingertips as he considered which pastry to buy. Then he'd get tea, black, not green, and sip it slowly while Mother and Amirah ate whatever pastries they chose. He wouldn't smile, not in public around strangers that he wouldn't ever know, but his eyes would be bright and warm over the top of his teacup as he watched them speculate about the recipes.

Another month and a half, that's all she had to wait. Amirah opened her eyes and laughed to see Calliope staring at her with a concerned frown. Hayden, her twin sister, was busy extolling the virtues of the raspberry donuts to a pair of tourists in heavy coats, thick gloves clutched in their hands and noses red from the cold outside.

Not that Amirah thought it was that cold. Not like home where it snowed ten months of the year and roasted the remaining two. She checked for anyone else coming in before coming to the cash register where

Calliope stood in her fairy-floss pink apron bedecked with delicate lace trim. The pink made Calliope stunningly beautiful, much as Calliope hated the color. It brought out the rose of her warm brown cheeks and made the spring of her lush dark curls seem even more pronounced.

"Why do you do that?" Calliope asked in a low enough voice that it wouldn't upset the tourists or make Hayden start teasing the two of them.

"Stop?" Amirah asked. When Calliope nodded while automatically beginning to prepare a green tea for her, Amirah laughed. "It smells like home. Well, not like home but the smells remind me of home. So I stop. I savor. This is a good thing, yes?"

Calliope blinked at her and then ducked her head to blush and smile and lick her lips as if she was searching for just the right thing to say. Anything she said would be welcome in Amirah's opinion but Calliope always seemed to want the exact word, the exact phrase to make Amirah laugh or smile.

Her beautiful eyes were more than enough for that in Amirah's opinion.

"Did you want a pastry, too?" Calliope asked just as she always did.

"Of course," Amirah said. "What's especially tasty today?"

"Everything," Calliope declared just a hair belligerently, as if someone had insulted their pastries before Amirah came in. "They're all good today."

"Then surprise me," Amirah replied and laughed at the way Calliope ducked her head to attempt to hide her blush. "I trust you. Whatever you think I will enjoy will be a delight."

The tourists pushed over, driving Amirah away from the cash register with that sort of wary scowl that she'd gotten used to since coming here. It could be her hijab, warm red and thick because of the weather lately. Or it could simply be that Amirah had dark skin and they had pale, pale skin and blond thin eyelashes. They certainly were short with Hayden as she took their money and in turn gave them the pastries, carefully wrapped in a paper bag emblazoned with Candy Courtship.

But they were gone moments later, leaving the three of them alone in the shop. Odd for it to be so empty at this time on a Friday but there was a cold front coming through and Amirah remembered hearing the boys in class talking about some big basketball game tonight. Or was it tomorrow? She couldn't remember and didn't truly care, not when there was a chance to flirt with Calliope and eat wonderful food.

"It'll be a minute for the tea," Calliope suggested so diffidently that Hayden rolled her eyes at her twin. "You can sit down."

"After I pay," Amirah said as she opened her purse. "Any leftover is for the tip, you understand. No change."

The eternal reminder made Hayden snort and then snicker at the way Calliope blushed and Amirah grin. Odd that she'd fallen for shy Calliope when Hayden's bright and forthright personality was so much more a match to her own. But not so odd really. Hayden was predictable. Calliope was always a challenge, always interesting, always exciting to interact with.

Twenty dollars exchanged hands and then Amirah went to sit next to the wall where the ovens radiated heat into the room. The little table was tucked behind a curio display full of tiny cupcakes, mugs and expensive chocolates that Amirah had paid for once and declared too good to eat. Though she did eat them from time to time, whenever Calliope's desire to treat Amirah exceeded her shyness about giving Amirah something extra-nice.

Four months had passed since Amirah first found Candy Courtship. They'd whirled by so quickly that Amirah could barely remember where each day had gone. The time she spent at school was always full of books and classes, studying for this test or that. It faded into a whirl that Amirah knew she would never sort out, no matter how hard she tried in the future.

Every moment she'd spent with Calliope, however, was crystal clear.

That first day Amirah had walked into Candy Courtship and Calliope had been running about, checking on patrons sitting at tables, her hair pulled up into a tight puff that bobbed with every movement. Amirah had licked her lips, walked on shaking legs to the counter and then completely failed to choose a pastry or a tea from the expansive menu.

Her eyes had been only for Calliope as she turned bright rose and ashen pale in turns.

"You gonna order or am I gonna deck you for bullying my twin?" Hayden had demanded, her jaw square and her dark eyes as hard as onyx as she glowered at Amirah.

"Bully?" Amirah had asked, blinking and then staring at Calliope's generous hips, those strong arms and the long dark curve of her neck as she bent to smile and giggle with a little girl who had frosting decorating her nose. "How could anyone bully such a beautiful woman?"

"Wait, what?" Hayden has asked, so stunned that she might have been the one 'decked'. "Are you serious?"

"Of course I am serious," Amirah had huffed. "I do not suppose there is a cell phone number I might ask for? Or something? Anything? How can I turn away and never see her again? She is the most beautiful woman I have yet seen in this city."

Hayden had burst out laughing and given Amirah a raspberry donut that was a meal by itself and a dry green tea for free just so that she could watch Calliope blush as Amirah tried and failed to flirt with her.

The first day was followed by a second and a third with similar results. It had taken Amirah nearly a month before Calliope stopped going pale when she caught Amirah staring at her. Two months had passed before the first time that Calliope dared to, very, very gently, flirt back.

It had been enough to make Amirah's heart sing with joy for days. Mother had quietly teased her about her lovely young lady when they talked on the phone. Father had chuckled and asked in an approving but teasing tone how Amirah would support Calliope and then hummed with interest when Amirah explained that Calliope was a businesswoman who supported herself quite well.

Yes, Amirah looked forward to bringing her parents to Candy Courtship. She wanted them to meet Calliope. More importantly, she wanted Calliope to meet her parents and to realize that no matter what tales she might have heard, she would be accepted and loved in Amirah's family.

"I thought you'd like to try one of our new pastries," Calliope said.

She brought not just the pastry but also two mugs. One held foamy-topped green tea for Amirah.

The other had whipped cream so apparently Hayden had told Calliope to take a break and eat with Amirah. Not that Calliope would usually eat their wares. No, those were for customers but hot chocolate appeared to be Calliope's exception much as iced coffee was for Hayden.

"It looks delicious," Amirah said, her eyes on Calliope's face, not the treat.

Calliope laughed, ducked her head and then tapped the table between them. "You haven't even looked at it yet. How could you tell?"

This time it was Amirah who ducked her head to hide a laugh. She shrugged and then pulled the pastry in front of her. Her hands froze as she saw a number written in icing on top of the very delectable looking slice of many-layered carrot cake.

Amirah's breath caught. She set her hands on either side of the carrot cake, the number running through her head over and over so that she would never, ever forget it. The firm press of her hands was the only thing that kept her hands from shaking. When she looked up Calliope was pale again, but smiling soft and shy and so gentle that it made Amirah's heart flip.

"Hayden said you wanted my phone number a long time ago," Calliope whispered. Her cheeks flared and she sipped her hot chocolate.

"I did," Amirah said. The words came out so strong, so confident that Calliope winced. "I do. I think I will never, ever forget it, no matter how long I live."

Calliope choked and then started laughing as the rosy blush spread until her whole face was red. "I doubt I'll have the number forever, silly."

"No, but it is a small part of you," Amirah said. "And I am grateful to be allowed it. May I... call you? That is the thing you say, yes? When you want to take someone on a date? Many dates?"

Calliope gasped and nearly rose even as Amirah caught her wrist and Hayden hissed at her to stay right where she was. Her wrist trembled under Amirah's hand as if she was terrified that something horrific would happen if she said yes.

"I do not know your language very well," Amirah continued because she could not lose her chance so soon after getting it. "I apologize if I offended you, Calliope. It is simply that I wish to spend time with you, learn more of you. A date is how this is done here, yes? At home I would ask my parents to speak to your parents but that is not possible, of course. They are at home and well, I do not know if you are close to your family."

Calliope sat with a thump in her chair that shook the table and nearly toppled both her hot chocolate and Amirah's green tea. Surprisingly, Hayden stared as well, as if she was stunned by Amira's words.

"This isn't just flirting," Calliope said so warily that Amirah carefully released her wrist. She nearly jumped when Calliope caught her hand and didn't let her pull back. "You really like me."

Amirah cocked her head to the left, frowning. "I do not know how to make it any more apparent but yes, I do. I have already told my parents of you. Mother wishes to share recipes with you and Hayden. Father admires that you have started your own business at such a young age, especially one so successful. My aunt thinks that the whole family should come visit but my uncle said that he fears scaring you off. I would spend... my whole life with you, should you wish it. I think I fell in love with you that first day as you laughed with the little girl with frosting on her nose and blushed every time you met my eyes."

The little speech tumbled out of Amirah's mouth. As she talked Hayden's smile grew and grew. Calliope's cheeks went so red that her ears began to blush and the rose drifted down her neck and then right on out to her wonderful strong arms and on down to her knuckles.

"I thought it was teasing," Calliope whispered. Her fingers trembled around Amirah's hand. "No one ever tells us we're beautiful."

"Then they are fools and idiots because you are stunning, both of you but you especially to my eyes," Amirah replied.

"I told you so!" Hayden crowed, punching the air and jumping up and down so vigorously that the pastry case rattled with the force of her impacts. "I told you she was crushing on you!"

Amirah laughed and shook her head at that, much to the apparent surprise of both Hayden and Calliope.

"Oh no, it is not a crush," Amirah said. She grinned. "My understanding is that crushes are small things, short-lived. That they will fade with time and distance. This. This is not a crush. I love you. I would be delighted to spend my life with you as my spouse. My wife. It will not fade or die. This I know."

Calliope gasped a laugh, tears rising to shine in her eyes. She shook her head before releasing Amirah's hand so that she could clasp her hands in front of her mouth. It took a moment before she could turn to Hayden who beamed at her, nodding so firmly that the many braids decorating her head flew around her cheeks.

"Then yes, you can call me," Calliope said. She smiled as her tears spilled over only to be brushed away quickly. "Or I could call you?"

"Let us eat and then after you close up shop I will take you out to dinner," Amirah said and her throat felt too tight, too hot with all the things she wanted to say now that it was finally allowed. "I know a wonderful little Persian restaurant that is open late.

I think you will like it. It, too, reminds me of home. I would... like to share some of myself with you."

Calliope grinned and picked up her hot chocolate. "I'd like that, too. It's slow. Maybe we can go early."

"Damn right you can!" Hayden exclaimed. "It's about damned time, too!"

Amirah laughed as Hayden turned away to greet the new guests who blew in out of the cold windy night. She looked and Calliope was staring aright at her as if Amirah was the greatest wonder of the world. It felt like flying for the first time, like taking the steering wheel of a car in her hands and pressing the accelerator when she was learning to drive. It was new and exciting and the most incredible sensation Amirah had ever had.

"I love you," Amirah whispered, leaning across the table so that they were nearly nose to nose. "I do. I truly do."

"I think..." Calliope whispered, glanced at the guests who couldn't quite see them tucked into the corner and then turned back with a shy smile, "I think I love you, too."

"Then I hope to have the rest of our lives to help you be certain of it," Amirah replied, her heart singing. "Drink. I will eat. We will run through the night and eat good food and I will give you my cell phone number. We will date. And someday, hopefully, we will marry and I will make you kahari and you will make me pastries and we will have children and grow old together."

Calliope laughed. She ran a finger over Amirah's cheek. "I'd like that. All of that. Together."

"Then it will be so," Amirah promised. "I will make it be for you, my beautiful Calliope."

The End

Author Bio

Meyari McFarland has been telling stories since she was a small child. Her stories range from adventures appropriate to children to erotica but they always feature strong characters who do what they think is right no matter what gets in their way.

Meyari has been married for just under twenty years and has no children or pets. She lives in the Puget Sound, WA and enjoys the fog, rain and cool weather that are typical here. When vacation times come, she and her husband usually go somewhere warm like Hawaii or they go on their own adventures to Japan and other far away countries.

Her life has included jobs ranging from cleaning motel rooms, food service, receptionist, building and editing digital maps, auditing and document control.

Other Books by Meyari McFarland:

Matriarchies of Muirin:
   Tales from the Dana Clanhouse
   Repair and Rebuild
   Storm Over Archaelaos
   Coming Together
   Facing the Storm
   Fitting In

Mages of Tindiere:
   Artifacts of Awareness
   Transplant of War
   City of the Dead

Debts to Recover:
   The Nature of Beasts

The Manor Verse:
   A New Path
   Following the Trail
   Crafting Home

   You can find these books and more at http://meyari.
wordpress.com/store/

Author's Note: I really love bold characters who charge through life making decisions with ease. Amirah is definitely one of those characters. She knows what she wants and she goes for it. Atif is another one of those characters. He's from one of my Manor Verse romance novels called Finding A Way. I thought you might enjoy a sample of Atif's story so here you go!

Finding A Way

1. Decisions

Dust. Atif sat in the pantry, eyes shut, and breathed. All he smelled was dust. His heart beat entirely too fast, making his empty stomach wobble enough that he wasn't sure if he'd be able to keep his meager breakfast down when he stood to walk outside. Between the fear, the hunger and the very quiet argument going on between Father and Mother, Atif didn't want to move.

The house was too quiet, not even the sound of the fire snapping and cracking on the other side of the house. Lord Ammad of Breding Manor had made sure that all the peasants in his district had mass heaters after last winter's horrible cold snap but they hadn't had the money to get fuel for the fire. Faez, Atif's second oldest brother, had worked so hard to cover their debts while Father was away but there wasn't enough left over now. Not that there had been before Father returned but at least then they'd had the option of promising payment when Father's goods sold.

There were no goods.

It had been weeks since they'd last had fresh fruit that Atif hadn't gathered himself. Their breakfast had been a gift from old Yoriko up the lane, just rice balls but it was more than Atif had eaten in days. Father had come back from his latest trip across the sea with nothing, not even his ship. He'd arrived in port on a Korean sailing ship in borrowed clothes because his ship, his beautiful trading ship, had crashed off Hokkaido.

Mother had gasped when he showed up at their door. She'd cried and clung to Father, pulled him into the house to cry some more where none of the neighbors could see.

They'd all cried at the loss of the crew. Half the town's sons had been on the ship, working for their share of the profits of the trip to Pakistan and back. Atif hadn't realized just how much things would change without the ship, without Father's trade goods, without hope.

"Haidar," Mother hissed. She never used to hiss at Father before the shipwreck. "We need to find some way to pay them."

"Sehr, if I had a way to pay them, I would have already done so," Father said and now his voice rose as another fight began. Too many fights lately, too.

"Contact Lord Ammad," Mother said for the thousandth time. "He's your cousin. He'll help!"

"He just put on a wedding," Father groaned. "Sehr, he doesn't have the money to help us right now."

Atif opened his eyes, staring at the door of the pantry. The little room was barely big enough for him to sit in with his knees pressed against his chest. It'd seemed much larger when Atif was a little boy. Then he would stare up at the shelves covered with preserves in their thick jars, at the bunches of herbs drying on pegs stuck in the rafters. Cheese and apples and big thick-hulled squash filled the little room with the promise of food to eat.

No herbs hung on the pegs now, other than one bedraggled strand of chives that had gotten stuck there and forgotten. He didn't share the floor with squash. No rice or grain sat in big baskets on the shelves. There weren't even beans waiting in dry wood boxes to be soaked and cooked until they were soft.

"Lady Shizuka is here!" Waqar called.

Atif stirred, stilled as Mother and Father's fight abruptly cut off and then waited until they stomped outside to greet their Lady. Then he stood and carefully slipped out of the pantry and into their bare little house.

The entire time he'd grown up Atif's house had been full of color. Mother had covered the bare wood floor with plush rugs from Pakistan. They'd had more rugs hung on the walls for insulation and more pillows to lounge on than anyone could need. Their kitchen had always had food waiting for someone to eat, either family or guests come to talk business with Father or Mother.

Now the rugs and pillows were gone. Only four thin blankets remained, carefully folded and stacked in a corner of the room. Everything had gotten sold, every single thing that they'd ever cherished, and it still wasn't enough for the family to survive. Atif sighed.

Arshia had married just before Father left on his doomed trip. She lived in a different village now and Atif was glad. At least she was doing well with her husband's family, potters that they were. Waqar had four jobs that he worked around the village. He worked so much that it had cost him his engagement to his sweetheart Saira. Faez worked, too, every other odd job the town had to offer. That left very little for Atif to do besides sit and listen and try to help.

Lady Shizuka smiled as she nodded at whatever grand claims Father was saying about getting back on their feet soon. She really was beautiful, long black hair and a round face that was the very image of the moon. Her wife, Lady Nabeela, stood behind her with an indulgent smile that made Atif want to scream. He could see the resemblance between Lady Nabeela and Father. Same beaked nose, same high cheekbones, same mop of heavy, wavy hair. Atif had the same nose, hair and eyes, too, just like his siblings.

Couldn't they see how desperate the situation was? But no, of course they couldn't. The outside of the house looked just like always, cedar planks painted in bright designs that mixed native Snohomish designs with traditional Muslim geometric patterns. Father had been so careful not to let their new poverty show outside the house.

"Hey, there you are, cousin," Lady Nabeela said. "Is there anything you need while we're here?"

Atif blinked at her, laughed quietly as he shook his head and then stared straight into her eyes with every bit of his desperation showing. "A job."

"Atif!" Mother gasped.

"We're not doing well," Atif snapped at her because no, he wasn't going to hide this anymore. They were starving to death and they didn't have to. "Father's ship went down and we lost everything other than the house, Lady Nabeela. My brothers are working every job available and there are no jobs left for me. Not in this village. I need a job that will give the family some hope of paying off our debts."

Lady Shizuka put a hand on Lady Nabeela's arm when she started and opened her mouth. The very shrewd look that Lady Shizuka gave Father made his chin come up and his lips go thin. Mother looked away and Waqar's shoulders slumped as he nodded confirmation.

Just putting the truth out there was like dropping a hundred pound weight from his back. Atif's head spun but that was probably the hunger. His hands shook and if he was lucky then it wouldn't matter that his desperation showed. Please let them do something to help the family!

"We don't need charity," Father growled finally.

"The debts are more than you can pay?" Lady Shizuka asked.

"At… this moment, yes," Father admitted with a frustrated sigh. "But we will pay them. We just need a little time"

Lady Shizuka nodded thoughtfully. "Then I know what Atif can do. He can become an apprentice like I did and learn a new trade that will help support the family into the future. There is a very large bonus given to the family when someone signs on. It should be enough to get you back on your feet. And, as he learns his new trade he will be able to send money home. Though I would not expect that you'll fall in love with a Lady somewhere and get married. That's quite rare, despite my circumstances."

Lady Nabeela clapped her free hand over her mouth but it did nothing to muffle her honk of laughter. Father stared at Lady Shizuka, then at Atif, his mouth open as if he was a frog getting ready to catch flies. Hope sent shivers up Atif's spine, down his arms, over his knees which shook so badly that he abruptly sat on the house steps.

Apprentice. He could apprentice. Atif had assumed that he'd work with Father on the ships or with Mother on selling the goods. It was the job that had seemed to lay in front of him since he was a tiny child. But that wasn't the only job in the world. He could learn a trade and establish a life somewhere else. Lady Shizuka was a doctor in addition to being a Lady and she'd learned that while she was an apprentice.

"I'll do it," Atif said. He waved at Mother's horrified gasp, Father's cursing. Even Waqar stared at him in horror. "I'll do it. What do I have to do? To sign? When can I start?"

"Come over to the carriage with me," Lady Shizuka said, patting Lady Nabeela's arm in such a warning way that Lady Nabeela snapped to attention and then stepped out of Lady Shizuka's way. "It's going to be hard. You won't be allowed direct contact with your family and you'll end up in a completely different part of the country, Atif. Let's talk in more detail before you make any final decisions."

Atif laughed as he stood, one hand on the doorframe so that his legs didn't give way again. His stomach growled so loudly that Lady Shizuka's brows drew together. He shook his head and then started towards the beautiful carriage with its dark-stained cedar body topped by a heavy canvas canopy. The horses were beautiful, spotted brown and gold and red with braided manes decorated with ribbons.

Every step he took from the house seemed to open Atif's world up. The dust and cold desperation bloomed into warmth from the horses, the scent of spiced meat buns somewhere in the carriage and the hint of fragrant cedar branches caught on the edges of the canopy. Atif found his shoulders straightening, his spine unrolling as if he was a fern in spring unfurling before the renewed warmth of the sun. Apprentice.

He didn't look back, didn't dare meet Mother's eyes and see the horror that had to be there. There was no way he could look at Father's shame. Or Waqar's embarrassment. They might never understand why Atif leaped at this opportunity but he knew it was the right choice. Come what may, his family needed help and this was something that only Atif could do.

He would become one of Their Majesties' apprentices. Somewhere, out in Ambermarle, he would be given a new home, a new name, and a new profession to learn. Doing this would save his family. If he was right, it might save their entire village because Father's ship had been what kept everyone going even if his trips took a year or more each time.

"I've already decided," Atif told Lady Shizuka. She blinked at him, head cocked to the side so that her waterfall of silky black hair tumbled over her shoulder. "How soon can I start?"

"Samurakami Haru-Sama!"

Haru didn't flinch at the shouted Japanese words though his not-quite run towards his mother's workshop did stumble as he stopped. He didn't allow himself to snarl, shout or keep going towards the smoke, the fire, the screams and cursing and horrifying moans that he knew he'd hear in his dreams tonight, as much as he wanted to.

Instead he took a deep breath, forced his shoulders down and his lips into an approximation of a pleasant, if harried, smile, and turned to face the representative of their Majesties. The woman was short, stern, her greying hair drawn back in two tight braids that hung as rigid over her shoulders as if they were made of stone.

Behind the officially nameless representative was a young man in an apprentice's white tunic and pants. Quite attractive, yes, if fairly wild-eyed and getting more so the longer Haru stared at him and yes, it was Haru's stare, not the chaos behind Haru if the young man's wide eyes locked onto Haru's face were anything to judge by. Haru switched his gaze to the representative and bowed, just barely, and hopefully it would be enough to convey that he was in a rather urgent hurry.

Though he would have thought that the smell of smoke, the, relatively, small explosion only moments ago and the rising cursing coming from his mother's workshop would be enough convey that.

"Please, do be welcome," Haru said. "I am afraid that I have an urgent matter," he waved towards the people running buckets of water into Mother's shop behind the heavy stone wall and thick not quite properly formal gate that served as Klallam Manor's official warning to tread carefully here, "that I must attend to. The servants will surely have tea prepared for you."

The representative's shoulders sagged slightly, so very slightly but it was as extreme on one of her type as if Haru had fallen over and begun to wail openly. "Again?"

"I am afraid Mother is determined to continue her experiments," Haru said. "Ren has not been successful in dissuading her."

"Lord Consort my ass," the representative muttered while glaring towards Mother's shop. "Go. We'll wait."

"My thanks," Haru said. "And my apologies."

He turned and ran towards Mother's shop with all the speed he could manage short of losing one of his sandals. The wall around her workshop had done its job. The explosion had, definitely, blown out every shoji screen in the smaller fabrication shops neighboring Mother's workshop but the shoji of the manor itself were intact. That was progress.

A story high and approximately twenty feet long, the new workshop that he'd ordered built after Mother burned down her last one, was surprisingly intact. The heavy stone walls were scorched, yes, but intact. And yes, the heavy redwood door that marked the entrance was lying on the ground like a ramp for fire fighters to run up but it looked as though it had come off its rails cleanly, leaving the building and the door solid. Still, he was cautious as he peeked inside to see just how bad the explosion damage was.

Thankfully she seemed to have been prepared this time. The majority of the explosion appeared to have been contained behind heavy redwood panels braced so that they wouldn't collapse instantly. Two at the far end of the workshop lay tumbled, burning, but the others were still in place. Everyone appeared to have been wearing the goggles Mother had invented so there shouldn't be any lost eyes and they all wore thick firemen jackets that dripped water so no one should be burned. It was hard to tell through the smoke and steam but no one looked as though they'd been hurt.

Still, as many times as she'd tried to get steam engines to work, as many explosions as he'd seen, Haru still found it hard to deal with the inevitable smoke, fire and scorch marks over everything and everyone. It smelled like death, the ash coating his tongue, his clothes, his very skin with that sense of doom that accompanied Mother's experiments.

"Mother?" Haru shouted over the firemen, the tinker who'd promised to help her one last time who now cursed at the top of his lungs between coughing fits and the, thankfully, falling crackle of flames hissing as a relay line of firemen threw buckets full of water into the blaze.

"Here!"

Haru followed the sound of her shout, then the lone arm waving in the cloud of smoke and steam. Lady Samurakami Jun of Klallam Manor sat on an old fuel bin that had been turned upside down, her sleek black hair now a frizzy, burnt mass on the right side of her face. It hung undamaged to her chin on the left side, giving her a lopsided appearance that prompted Haru to sigh.

"Good news?" Mother asked with such wryness that Haru shook his head and laughed. "Ah. Not good news."

"Their Majesties' representative is outside with our new apprentice, Mother," Haru said. "I believe they arrived just in time for the explosion."

Mother groaned. Her head sagged towards her chest as her hands flopped on top of her knees. Which,

Haru knew, meant that she'd completely forgotten that the new apprentice was due to arrive today. And that there was to be an audit in the next week, at the latest assuming the auditor had bad traveling weather instead of their current wonderful weather. Possibly she had also forgotten that she had Court to attend tomorrow with several major legal cases to adjudicate.

Someone, probably Haru's twin brothers Michi and Kaoru, threw open the great doors at the far end of the workshop that had come ajar but not opened all the way. Air rushed in, covering Haru with smoke-scented steam, before flowing right back out in a rush that sounded like the suck of the tide over the gravel in the bay. At least it cleared the air so that Haru's nose wasn't filled with fire and scorched hair.

"Are you injured?" Haru asked because with Mother there was no telling. Sometimes she thought a paper cut was the worst injury possible and yet when he was twelve she'd burned her left elbow so badly that the skin blackened and she had barely slowed down.

"No, just scorched," Mother sighed. "All right. If you'll escort them inside, I'll make sure everyone is intact here. I can figure out what went wrong later."

"You'll actually come in within the hour, yes?" Haru asked and didn't flinch in the slightest when Mother glowered at him. "If you need to do the analysis immediately, then say so. I'd rather have an accurate estimate of your arrival time than keep putting them off.""

Her mouth twisted as if she'd bitten into an imported lemon but she nodded as she stood and swayed. Haru automatically put one hand under her elbow to keep her from falling. It was still strange to be taller than Mother. She was such a personality that for her to be barely up to his chin felt odd. Wrong. And yet, there he was, staring down at the top of her head where the part of her hair neatly divided shriveled remnants from smoke-filled healthy strands.

"You'll have to shave your head again," Haru sighed.

"Good," Mother said, grinning up at him as if that was the best thing she'd ever heard. "I look better with no hair, no matter what everyone else says."

Haru swallowed a laugh and then let her go, estimate on arrival time undelivered. Right. She'd show up when she showed up, probably when Michi and Kaoru dragged her in by the wrists to make her sit, eat and get cleaned up. He would never figure out how Mother ended up as a Lady when she was so desperately unsuited for it.

Lady she was though, for all that she pushed the majority of her duties off on Haru at every opportunity, including Their Majesties' representative and the new apprentice with his velvet brown skin, hair like the waves on the bay in a storm at night and eyes that stared at everyone in obvious shock. Haru brushed himself off as he walked back to them, more slowly this time.

"I am afraid she will be delayed," Haru said and then spread his hands at the representative's irritated expression. "I can, of course, take responsibility for the new apprentice if you are in a hurry. Mother is likely to be several hours assessing what happened in this latest failure."

Their Majesties' representative pressed her lips together as she glared towards the workshop. At least the fire appeared to be out. Haru saw only steam rising out of the windows and doors when he glanced over his shoulder. The smell of the ash lingered though, filling Haru's mouth and nose.

"Klallam Manor formally accepts him?" the representative asked with an admirable level of calm given that she looked as though she wanted to stride into Mother's workshop and shake Mother until her teeth came loose.

"We do," Haru said with a properly slow, serious bow to the older woman. "With gratitude. I will do my best to ensure Mother does not immediately coopt him into her research."

The representative sighed and nodded, patted the apprentice on the shoulder before striding off to her very stern-looking basic black carriage. She swung into the back and the driver shook the reins smartly, startling the horses into a quick trot that carried them away so fast that it was as if they wanted to escape.

And perhaps they did. Haru sighed. The apprentice swallowed audibly when Haru turned and smiled at him. Obviously not one of his best smiles.

"Well, not the introduction I would have wished for you but perhaps more accurate to our daily life at Klallam Manor," Haru said. He gestured for the apprentice to follow him inside the gate to Klallam Manor.

Unlike the gate to Mother's workshop, composed of huge logs barely stripped of their bark, the gate into Klallam Manor was a work of art. Deliberately. Grandfather had put up proper Japanese torii when he rebuilt the Manor on traditional Japanese plans. They'd been huge, towering three stories over people who entered, painted bright red and quite impressive. Haru had always liked them.

But the wet weather and time had eaten away at the base of the torii so that it was unstable. That had allowed Haru to replace the grand logs with something more appropriate to Ambermarle and Klallam Manor's place in society. He'd commissioned three great cedar trees to be cut from the nearby forest and then had local artists carve them in the native style as though they were totem.

It was a very fitting look as far as Haru was concerned. The gate had the shape of a torii, tying in with the ruling family's ancestry, but the appearance of something native, something Snohomish. He truly did like the red and white accents that outlines the various bears, wolves, eagles, moose and orca decorating the gate.

Other people's objections to the 'bastardization of tradition' were unimportant, especially given that Mother had already said that she liked it.

"I am Samurakami Haru," Haru said to the apprentice with a little bow and a wave to follow him through the gate, "heir to Lady Samurakami Jun, she of the explosion you just witnessed."

"Ah, please call me um, Atif?" the apprentice asked, waving one hand towards Mother's workshop. Odd to have a proper name from an apprentice but perhaps it was one he'd always wanted. Most apprentices took more fanciful names for the duration of their training. "Is she okay?"

"Oh yes," Haru said. He chuckled at the pure disbelief on Atif's face. "Truly, she is. There would be far more swearing if she were not. I am afraid that my mother is quite devoted to her experimentation. She is in the process of developing a steam engine to power ship travel across the ocean. It is not yet successful but given Mother's determination we expect that she will find a solution to her pressure problems sometime in the next few years."

"Steam engine?" Atif asked, stopping dead in his tracks to stare at Haru. He was slightly shorter than Haru, with thick eyebrows that drew together dramatically. "For ships? It would... power oars?"

"Mother thinks that wheels," Haru said, gesturing his hands like the paddles of a water wheel, round and round, "would be most effective. Her assistant has created several small scale models that appear quite promising though they work on springs, not steam. If they're right ships might be able to make the trip to Japan in oh, weeks instead of months."

Atif choked, turned and stared out the main gate of Klallam Manor with all its formal frippery carved into the great logs towards Mother's shop. "My father was a sailor until his ship went down. He could make so many trips if it only took weeks. It would change commerce everywhere throughout the world."

"It would, indeed," Haru agreed. He gently touched Atif's elbow, smiling softly at the way the young man started. "If she can stop the boiler from exploding. So far she has not found a method to do that which is not too expensive in terms of weight and material costs. The amount of metal needed is quite harmful to the environment. Mining so much would radically change the mountains. She is still working on it, though. I imagine in time she will find some method that works without too much cost."

This time when Haru turned and gestured for Atif to follow, he did, down the covered path to the main entrance, stopping to remove his sandals along with Haru and then with Haru as he continued onwards towards the apprentice quarters. Two steps behind Haru and to the right, as was proper. Difficult for conversation but then Haru didn't suppose that conversation was desired at the moment. He had to stink of smoke and ash.

A proper tour of the Manor would have to wait until Haru didn't feel like he trailed mother's chaos behind him like ashy footprints that would never wash away. The last thing he wanted to do was stain the lovely native art that decorated the walls, ceilings and floors with ashes. Still, Atif did get to see into the formal hall where Mother held court. Or more accurately, where Haru normally held court because Mother forgot and couldn't be torn away from her experiments. The shoji screens around the inner room and the dais had been pulled back to air the tatami mats out. It looked empty rather than grand.

Haru turned right, leading Atif through the covered walkway towards the kitchen and its connection to the apprentice quarters. Most of the shoji were open in the offices and thankfully no one looked too disturbed by the latest explosion. They bowed as Haru passed, eyes glancing over Atif before they returned to work. Apparently the wall they'd built around Mother's workshop had done its work better than Haru expected. As close as the offices were to her, the shoji should be torn and the staff terrified but not today.

It had made the offices on the north side nearest Mother darker but the safety was worth it. Haru found his shoulders relaxing as they continued onwards to the kitchen and the entrance to the apprentice quarters. Thankfully the shouts and cursing from behind Mother's wall had subsided into a busy murmur of voices that Haru recognized as intensive problem solving. Little hope that she would emerge before nightfall if they'd already reached that stage of discussion.

"You'll find the Manor relatively easy to navigate, I hope," Haru said. "Mother's workshop is completely self-contained. To enter it you would have to go back through the main gate and then through the gate you saw. We find it to be much safer that way."

"I can see why," Atif said with a little laugh that sounded so shaky that Haru paused at the door to the kitchen to look over his shoulder at the young man. "That was... shocking."

"I know," Haru said. "Truly, I do apologize. Mother was told that you were to arrive today but I suspect she forgot in her enthusiasm. It happens fairly frequently, I'm afraid. I'll do what I can to get you assigned somewhere not prone to explosions right away, unless you want the excitement."

"No!" Atif exclaimed, hands up to ward that off. "No, thank you. I'd prefer no explosions at all if possible."

"Good," Haru said, amused. "I can definitely use help with the actual work of ruling our lands, Atif. Mother enlists virtually everyone in her experiments, even my younger brothers Michi and Kaoru. This will likely be a place you spend a great deal of time. This is the kitchen. Access to the apprentice quarters is strictly through here so you'll be coming through many times a day."

Finding A Way is now available at all major retailers in ebook and TPB format.

Afterword

I truly love romantic stories. There's something wonderful about two people coming together, realizing that they care about each other and then deciding that they'll make their lives together. Love is such an important part of life that writing stories about it makes me happy.

It's also nice getting to write stories where people just accept non-straight love. Amirah's family is one of those families, one of the sort that I wish existed all over the place. They love her, accept her and wouldn't dream of wishing she'd change to be more conventional.

Hopefully someday in the future this story will seem boring and mundane. Amirah's family should be so average as to be invisible. Sadly, the world we live in hasn't reached this level yet.

Here's hoping that it won't be too much longer before they are the normal. Thank you for reading—I hope you enjoyed the story!

Meyari McFarland
October, 2015
http://meyari.wordpress.com/

17550851R00030

Printed in Great Britain
by Amazon